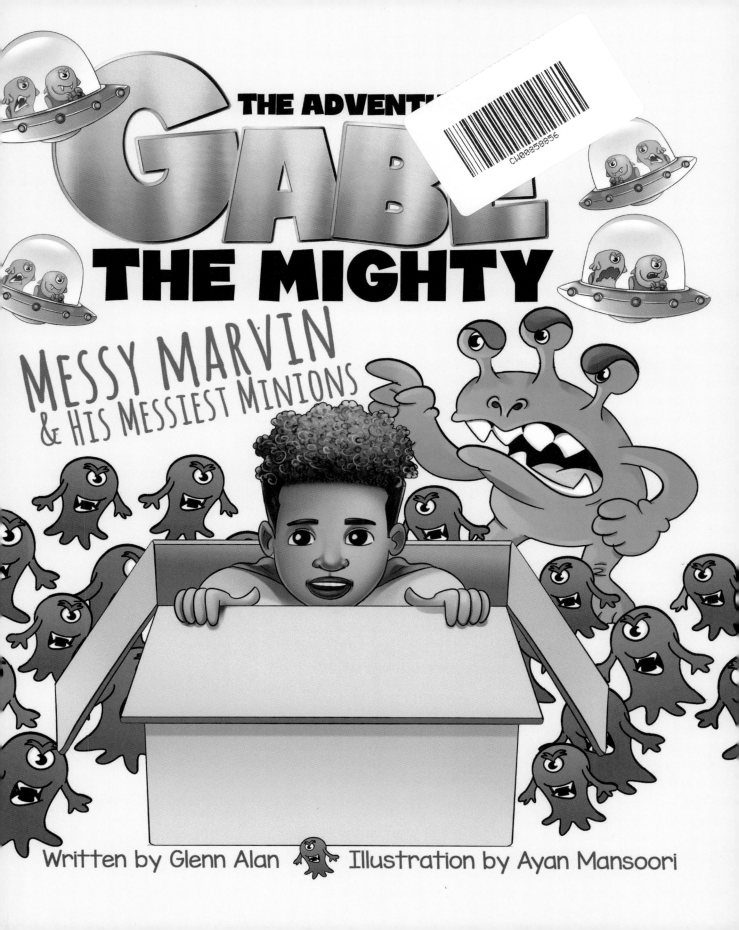

THE ADVENTURES OF GABE THE MIGHTY

MESSY MARVIN & HIS MESSIEST MINIONS

Written by Glenn Alan   Illustration by Ayan Mansoori

THIS BOOK WAS INSPIRED BY THE ALMOST, NEARLY TRUE, A LITTLE EXAGGERATED STORIES OF GABRIEL KINNARD-BROWN

Copyright © 2021 Glenn Alan

Illustrated by Ayan Mansoori
Editor: DeJuan Mason
Educational Consultants:
August Bullock, Amber Campbell, Jennifer Lipford Petticolas & Shandell Richards

All rights reserved. This book or any portion thereof may not be reproduced or used in any manner whatsoever without the express written permission of the publisher except for the use of brief quotations in a book review.

Printed in the United States of America.

Imprint Publishing Group
600 Pennsylvania Ave SE
PO Box 15341
Washington, DC 20003

www.GabeTheMighty.com

IMPRINT
PUBLISHING GROUP

THE ADVENTURES OF
GABE
THE MIGHTY

MESSY MARVIN
& HIS MESSIEST MINONS

TODAY'S SUPERPOWER IS
RESPONSIBILITY
RESPONSIBILITY MEANS DOING THE THINGS YOU ARE SUPPOSED TO DO AND ACCEPTING THE RESULTS OF YOUR ACTIONS.

It must be the weekend because I can hear loud music coming from the living room.

My mom always plays music on weekend mornings. She says, "The music helps the family to get in the mood to do chores."

The only mood I get from weekend chore music, is the mood to hide under the covers and pretend like it's Messy Monday.

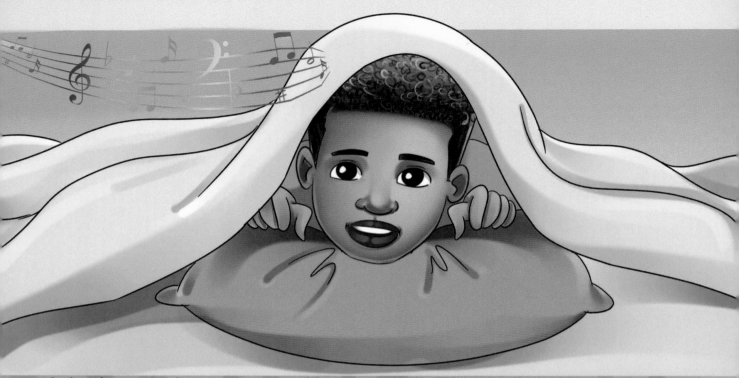

Weekend chores are the worst. It means that I have to clean up my room before I can go outside and play.

I like when my room is messy. It's comfortable when everything is out in the open.

"Gabe, your room is a mess," my mom tells me.
"Cleaning your room is your responsibility."

"It's supposed to be a mess," I say. "If it wasn't, then it wouldn't be Messyville. The messiest planet in the universe. The home of Messy Marvin and his Messiest Minions."

As soon as mom closes my bedroom door, Messy Marvin and his Messiest Minions appear.

"Capture that kid before he cleans up our planet,"
Messy Marvin yells.

I jump out of my bed, I mean my Rocketship and race over to the closet to put on my super cape and my G-shield, and become...

Laser beams are shooting all around me. A thousand Messy Minions. No, a million... all with one thing in mind - to capture Gabe The Mighty.

PEW, PEW, PEW, PEW!

"Get him!" One of the Messy Minions says.

"He's too fast," says another one.

"He must be using his super speed."

PEW, PEW, PEW, PEW!

I SLIDE...

AND HIDE!

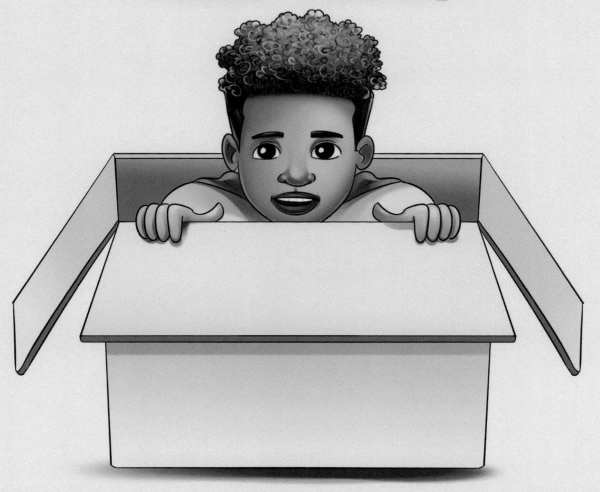

AND PUT MY TOYS AWAY.

If I make one wrong move, I will be toast - the burnt yucky kind.

Suddenly, the Messy Minions have me cornered. I am outnumbered - six million to one.

COULD THIS BE THE END OF GABE THE MIGHTY?

"We got you now, Gabe The Nighty," Messy Marvin says. "This planet will always be the messiest planet in the universe!"

"That's Gabe The Mighty to you, Mr. Messy Marvin," I say. Then I pull out my super secret odor eliminator, and with one spray...

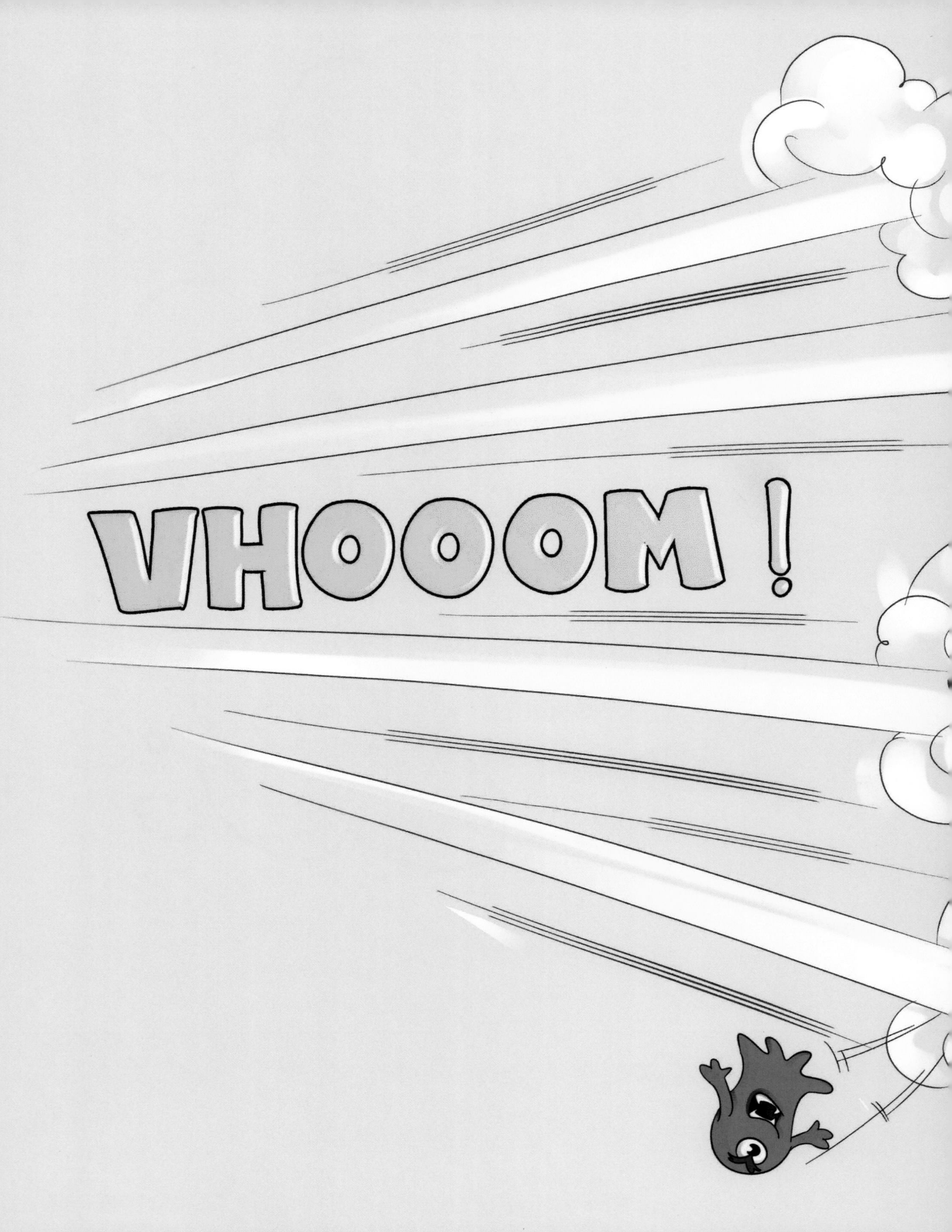
VHOOOM!

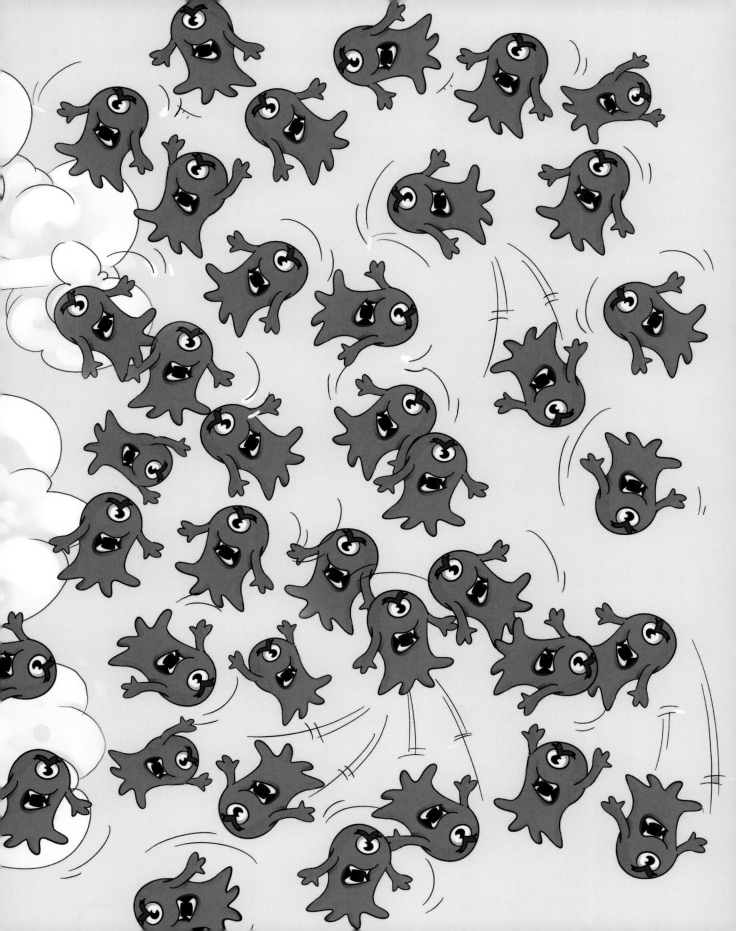

I clean the whole planet.

Just another job for Gabe The Mighty!

HOW DO YOU USE RESPONSIBILITY AS YOUR SUPERPOWER?

About the Author

Glenn Alan is an award-winning author, poet, playwright, and arts advocate. He has over three decades of experience in the areas of education, juvenile justice, and art as therapy.

Glenn is also a champion for children with incarcerated parents and a founding member of the National Center for Juvenile Justice Reform and the DC Black Theatre & Arts Festival.

Join the journey at
GabeTheMighty.com
and discover the superpower in you.

This Book Belongs to:

_____

My Superpower is:

_____

Printed in Great Britain
by Amazon

71141112R00020